SERIOUS Flash

Ben Warden is the editor of the much-loved Serious Flash Fiction Project. With significant support from Katie Clark and Isa Asbury, this 11th volume is brought to you with great devotion to the contributors.

Selection & Editing by Ben Warden
Pre-selection by Katie Clark
2025 Social Media Campaign by Isa Asbury

To tiny adventures, colour + wonderful worlds

Serious Flash Fiction

This collection is a compilation of the winning entries from the *Serious Flash Fiction* competition 2025.

DEDICATION

To Marilyn – thank you for the colour.

CONTENTS

THE CHALLENGE

With it's origins in Twitter, the Serious Flash Fiction project challenges people to create a story in the character limit of a tweet. The competition sets no themes or restrictions, but the story must fit the 140 character limit when the project was started in 2013 and expanding in 2018. Now spanning platforms, the competition retains it's character limit of under 270 characters (around 45-50 words).

Ben Warden first found flash fiction on Twitter in 2013, while researching writing forms. Despite the incredible character restriction, Ben was overwhelmed by the wealth and diversity of the stories being generated. As a lover of storytelling, Ben found the form fascinating and wanted to create a way to get more writers and readers involved.

It was at this point that he decided to launch a competition in support of flash fiction and a year later, after much encouragement from the winners of volume one, chose to use Amazon's self-publishing platform to create a physical anthology of the best works entered.

Serious Flash Fiction has been running for twelve years, with eleven anthologies published. The project aims to inspire creativity, offer an accessible platform for new and existing voices and encourage experimentation and play.

INTRODUCTION

Well, this is the eleventh introduction and you'd think we were running out of things to say! I'll be honest, I almost forgot we had to write one of these this year!? But, 2025 has been an interesting year for Serious Flash Fiction. We finally decided to step back from our Twitter homeland and branch out into Instagram/accepting your stories through our website. And, I'm very glad we did. Whatever my, your, Great Aunty Edith's political views, what I can tell you is we've only received about 15% of the entries this year through X. Wow.

It genuinely made me really sad to know our beautiful writing community is slowly disbanding. But guess what? We found a host of you on Instagram. So, haha capitalist tides, you won't break us!

On a slightly sobering side though, we have had to start our social media presence again. After 12 years of building our crew, we'll be finding you all, posting new content and trying to get traction for the second time. So, I end this year with a little request. Please, if you enjoy this book and enjoy the project. Find us on Instagram at @serious_flash_fiction and help us shout about this brilliant project and all the fantastic contributors.

And thank you, as always, for your stories, support and your time. We love you – mushy, but true.

VOLUME XI

Scales discarded. Salty and rusty. A pair of new feet, beach-washed. Ready to explore. One foot raised, another sunken in sand. A dainty footprint. Dripping golden. She made another. And another. In the hope he would find her. And welcome her to his world.

By Roopa Raveendra

I sprinkle a circle of salt around my lips to protect us all from the ghosts in my throat. The spectres of my past sometimes slip out. So now I clench my teeth, make them retreat. Look close, you'll see them haunting me, behind my eyes.

By Daniela Nunnari

Tulips nod spring heads over the mound.

By summer, the sun brittles the soil, teasing a reveal of what lies below. The fall winds almost whip the police writ from my hand, but as the winter snow rolls in, halting the excavation, I smile.

Winter always was my favourite.

By Estelle Tudor

A mechanical sound. Repeating.
Like that train who said I think I can. Over again.
The washing machine turns. Makes it cycle.
I fold laundry to the rhythm. Breath in time.
Find a single sock. Unmatched. Detached. Forgotten.
Like our yesterday.

By Becky Spence

One morning, the Earth shivered and cracked.
Peeling back layers like old skin. Mountains folded, seas
slipped away - revealing new lands untouched.
Strange people stepped forward, not born but
remembered, as if time had simply paused them.
The world, reborn, exhaled.

By Isra Noor

She shrank with each second, 15 minutes after the
Q injection, her body compressing.
Memories flashed—her parents' divorce, the crash, the kid
dying, the Europa penal colony sentence.
Her tears streamed, time sped by, and she escaped...
with her thoughts.

By Zary Fekete

As the plane vanishes from the radar, lost to the ancient mystery of the Bermuda Triangle, somewhere a girl drops her sea blue crayon and picks up her favorite, outrageously orange.
She furiously colours each tentacle of the giant kraken as it reaches towards the sky.

By Daniela Nunnari

What does he be waiting for? He sits by the river all day long, eyes fixed on the water as it flows through his toes. His eyes never move. Never have I ever seen him anywhere else, but I think he enjoys the skies white beard, and the river's whiskers on a windy day.

By Ronan Collins

A Spring day. Almost summer in appearance. Sat at my desk. A bumble bee flies in the window, for the third time. I wonder what it wants, where it's going. This bee. So keen to say hello. I long to reach out and fly away. On its wings. On a dream. Far from here.

By Becky Spence

In the trenches of Malon IV, Guardsman Kael aimed his lasgun at the Tyranid charging through smoke. One shot— lucky, true—pierced its eye. As it fell, silence. Then a screech. Ten more crawled from the dark. Kael sighed, reloaded, and whispered, "Emperor, watch me."

By Mighty Shadow

A girl and her toy crossed the man in a hood.

A lady and her briefcase crossed the man in a hood.

A mother and her daughter crossed the man in a hood.

A grandmother and her daughter-in-law crossed the man in a hood.

By Chiemeziem Everest Udochukwu

In the hollow of the cannon, the sad clown waits. Someday, he'll achieve escape velocity and crash through the big top. Only when he sees the clouds will his frown turn into a smile. Until then, this small moment of hope is his only consolation.

By A. A. Rubin (@TheSurrealAri)

The world was full of boring bastards and Martin was, without doubt, the most prosaic man in all England. But today he would do something astonishing...
the breaking news came at precisely 10.27am.

By Derek Jennings

The sun rose, casting golden glances across the sky, hoping to catch a glimpse of her. But they only met for a breath at dawn & dusk—fleeting touches of light & shadow. The moon lingered, leaving silver kisses on the edge of his light. The sky painted in his blush.

By Isra Noor

Theirs was a winter love story, hers and her snowman's. The same one with button eyes and a stick nose, always standing by the street bench, waiting for her. They exchanged frosty kisses on winter evenings until the spring sun came calling.

By Roopa Raveendra

He rested his elbows on the open window frame and stared. Blank eyes took in nothing. He visualized his room, the woman, her pleading, his life, noting every detail and committing it to memory. He spent the rest of his night destroying all of her things.

By Mark Binmore

Gerald pressed "Input" for the sixth time. The TV blinked, then resumed its silence. "Try channel 3," Doris offered, eyes narrowed. Somewhere, the DVD menu played endlessly. They would never watch Midsomer Murders, but they'd died trying.

By Micheal Lee

The world ended just as it began - in silence. No fire, no flood, just a hush, like breath held too long. And in that stillness, stars blinked open, the void yawned wide, and darkness waited, just as it had before the first word was spoken.

By Isra Noor

The Script Room was in chaos.

The Writers in an uproar.

Desks pounded, keyboards slammed.

Blank, frozen screens.

Servers down, systems crashed.

Data wiped.

Cyber attack.

Studio bosses furious.

Screams and curses.

They had completely lost the plot.

By Mr Bartholemew (@DrZorbas)

"Get to the deck!" The ship shook as I rushed.
Icelandic winds fought me as I pushed the door, feeling my
way out. The darkest night I'd ever seen, guided by the
bright lights of the stars. I look up, seeing green and white
playfully dancing across the sky.

By Sarah R. New

When I am with you, there is no racing heart.
No sweaty palms, no darting eyes, no wrong words.
There is ivy growing, the sun rising, rivers quietly bubbling.
Butterflies dance from stem to stem, hoping to find a fit place.
I have found mine between your arms.

By Daphne (@DPwriting)

Trudging home through the blackout, she saw her husband
smiling at her in his sheepskin flight jacket.
Before she could speak, he disappeared.
She didn't believe her eyes;
his plane had been missing for a week.
In the morning, a telegram came. He was in Stalag Luft 3.

By KJ Mansfield

Language was an unseen, yet ever-present barrier. But my grandmother never let that stop me from feeling her love. Just her standing on the other side of a car window as we pulled away each year, hand on glass, lip trembling with all the words she could never say.

By Jenny Wong (@jenwithwords)

I had never met a person that was a
door-to-door onion seller.
The stories they knew would bring tears to your eyes.

By Reben Paint

It's said ravens scratch their mates as a sign of affection.
I return your gaze with a soft, claw-like embrace.
Three ravens arrive, one by one, like water droplets before
the ceiling caves. Then comes Unkindness. Flesh pricked
with feathers. A fusion of beak and bone.

By Harriet Fletcher

From Hell's heart, Ahab stabs at the whale, but despite his
unholy devotion, his pursuit remains futile.
For the whale swims different seas in the afterlife, clear
seas, free of blood and harpoons, far out of reach from the
depths of the pit where Ahab's soul resides.

By A. A. Rubin (@TheSurrealAri)

Slinks in late, throwing kisses like hand grenades. Huffs away at my rebuff. I hear the upending of photographs, the shatter of an ornament, a disturbing quiet. He's up at four pacing and glaring at walls. When morning hits me, he's curled up at the foot of the bed.

By Alex Callaghan

My grandmother, in all her young beauty, pauses to open a door in 1905. I like to imagine I'm on the other side asking to see her garden and to discuss her favorite flowers. Just girls together in another century.

By Debbie Robson (@lakelady2282)

IF YOU GOT THIS FAR...

Thank you!

If you've enjoyed this anthology, please consider giving us a review on amazon, finding and following the brilliant contributors, or giving us a follow:

@Serious_Flash_Fiction on Instagram

@FlashSerious on X

Editor Ben Warden:

@Ben_Warden – on X and Instagram

Printed in Dunstable, United Kingdom